Santa's Stowaway

BRANDON DORMAN

Greenwillow Books
An Imprint of HarperCollinsPublishers

Digital art was used to prepare the full-color art.

The text type is 22-point Aldine 401.

Library of Congress Cataloging-in-Publication Data

Dorman, Brandon.

Santa's stowaway / by Brandon Dorman.

p. cm.

"Greenwillow Books."

Summary: Santa's newest elf hides on the sleigh and accompanies Santa

on his rounds to see for himself what makes Christmas so special.

ISBN 978-0-06-135188-4 (trade bdg.)

[1. Christmas—Fiction. 2. Elves—Fiction. 3. Santa Claus—Fiction.] I. Title.

PZ7.D727596San 2009   [E]—dc22   2009006187

09 10 11 12 13 First Edition LEO 10 9 8 7 6 5 4 3 2

 Greenwillow Books

For my V-man Sam

It was Christmas Eve in Santa's workshop.

"Ho, ho, ho! Gather round," said Santa to the elves.

"It's time for the final inspection."

Sam was excited. It was his first year working in the toy shop, and he couldn't wait to show Santa what he had made.

"Superb work," said Santa. "Your jack-in-the-box made me jump, and this spyglass is spectacular."

"Thank you, Santa." Sam smiled. Then he stepped aside to show Santa one last toy.

A doll sat propped up on Sam's workbench.
"I've lost one of the buttons for her dress," Sam said.
"Don't worry, Sam," said Santa, chuckling softly.
"You've done a fine job. She's perfect just as she is."
Sam sighed with relief. But as Santa turned to leave,
Sam asked, "Santa, why do we work so hard making
all the toys? Why does Christmas matter?"

A light began to sparkle in Santa's eyes. He leaned toward Sam and whispered, "You'll have to find that out for yourself."

Then Santa stood tall and shouted to the elves, "Ho, ho, ho! Congratulations to you all! These are the finest toys I've ever seen. Now it's time to load the sleigh!"

Sam turned back to the doll with the missing button. "Do you know what makes Christmas so special?" he whispered. But the doll didn't answer.

Suddenly Sam had an idea. A wonderful, perfect idea.

While Santa thanked his helpers, Sam slipped
into the sleigh and hid behind Santa's seat.

Soon Santa climbed into the sleigh. Sam heard the crack of the reins, then they were racing through the sky. "Ho, ho, ho!"

Sam smiled. Santa's reindeer were graceful, and flying was wonderful. Was this what made Christmas special?

The sleigh started to slow down, flying lower and lower until it landed softly on a rooftop. Santa grabbed a giant bag of toys and disappeared down the chimney. What was Santa doing? All at once, Santa popped out of the chimney and jumped back into the sleigh. "Onward!" he shouted to the reindeer.

As they flew from house to house, Sam wanted to ask Santa how he kept going up and down the chimneys. Was it magic? What did he do when he was inside the house? How did Santa know which toys to deliver?

But Sam stayed hidden, except to
peek at the moonlit streets below.

Sam decided he had to find out what Santa was doing. As soon as the sleigh landed on the next roof, Sam crept into Santa's bag. He felt Santa lift the sack and then heard a quiet *swoosh* as they slid down the chimney.

Sam looked around in amazement.
Santa was putting presents under a
beautiful tree. Sam watched him fill
the stockings with toys and treats.
Just as Santa finished, Sam
thought he heard a noise . . .

In the doorway
stood a girl.

"You're up late, little one," Santa whispered softly. He took one more toy out of his bag and handed it to her.

Sam couldn't believe it. It was the doll he had made. As the girl cradled her gift she quietly said, "She's perfect."

Sam ducked out of sight
as Santa lifted the bag and
backed into the fireplace.
"Merry Christmas,"
Santa whispered.
"Merry Christmas!"

When the last present had been delivered and the reindeer had turned toward home, Santa laughed and looked over his shoulder.

"You're very clever, my little friend," he said. "You see, Sam, each year one curious elf stows away on my sleigh, to discover what makes Christmas so special.

Did you find your answer?"

Sam remembered all of the hard work
and love he had put into the toys he had made.
And he thought about the girl holding her new
doll. He would never forget her smile.

And at that moment Sam understood, and a light
sparkled in *his* eyes. "Oh, yes!" he said to Santa.
"Merry Christmas!"